AWARDED

THE CALDECOTT MEDAL

AS

"The most distinguished American picture book for children"

IN THE YEAR OF ITS PUBLICATION

Also by Robert McCloskey

LENTIL

HOMER PRICE

CENTERBURG TALES

BLUEBERRIES FOR SAL

ONE MORNING IN MAINE

TIME OF WONDER

BURT DOW: DEEP-WATER MAN

MAKE WAY FOR DUCKLINGS

By ROBERT McCLOSKEY

THE VIKING PRESS · NEW YORK

Mr. and Mrs. Mallard were looking for a place to live. But every time Mr. Mallard saw what looked like a nice place, Mrs. Mallard said it was no good. There were sure to be

foxes in the woods or turtles in the water, and she was not going to raise a family where there might be foxes or turtles. So they flew on and on.

When they got to Boston, they felt too tired to fly any further. There was a nice pond in the Public Garden, with a little island on it. "The very place to spend the night," quacked Mr. Mallard. So down they flapped.

Next morning they fished for their breakfast in the mud at the bottom of the pond. But they didn't find much.

Just as they were getting ready to start on their way, a strange enormous bird came by. It was pushing a boat full of people, and there was a man sitting on its back. "Good morning," quacked Mr. Mallard, being polite. The big bird was too proud to answer. But the people on the boat threw peanuts into the water, so the Mallards followed them all round the pond and got another breakfast, better than the first.

"I like this place," said Mrs. Mallard as they climbed out on the bank and waddled along. "Why don't we build a nest and raise our ducklings right in this pond? There are no foxes and no turtles, and the people feed us peanuts. What could be better?"

"Good," said Mr. Mallard, delighted that at last Mrs. Mallard had found a place that suited her. But—

"Look out!" squawked Mrs. Mallard, all of a dither. "You'll get run over!" And when she got her breath she added: *"This is no place for babies, with all those horrid things rushing about. We'll have to look somewhere else."*

WEEBK!

So they flew over Beacon Hill and round the State
House, but there was no place there.

They looked in Louisburg Square, but
there was no water to swim in.

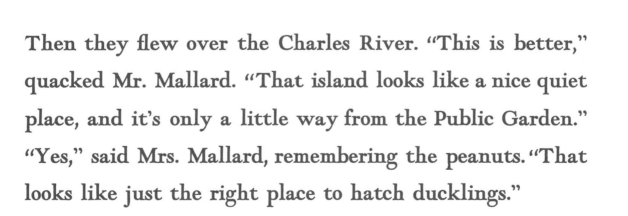

Then they flew over the Charles River. "This is better," quacked Mr. Mallard. "That island looks like a nice quiet place, and it's only a little way from the Public Garden." "Yes," said Mrs. Mallard, remembering the peanuts. "That looks like just the right place to hatch ducklings."

So they chose a cozy spot among the bushes near the water and settled down to build their nest. And only just in time, for now they were beginning to molt. All their old wing feathers started to drop out, and they would not be able to fly again until the new ones grew in.

But of course they could swim, and one day they swam over to the park on the river bank, and there they met a policeman called Michael. Michael fed them peanuts, and after that the Mallards called on Michael every day.

After Mrs. Mallard had laid eight eggs in the nest she couldn't go to visit Michael any more, because she had to sit on the eggs to keep them warm. She moved off the nest only to get a drink of water, or to have her lunch, or to count the eggs and make sure they were all there.

One day the ducklings hatched out. First came Jack, then Kack, and then Lack, then Mack and Nack and Ouack and Pack and Quack. Mr. and Mrs. Mallard were bursting with pride. It was a great responsibility taking care of so many ducklings, and it kept them very busy.

One day Mr. Mallard decided he'd like to take a trip to see what the rest of the river was like, further on. So off he set. "I'll meet you in a week, in the Public Garden," he quacked over his shoulder. "Take good care of the ducklings."

"Don't you worry," said Mrs. Mallard. "I know all about bringing up children." And she did.

She taught them how to swim and dive.

She taught them to walk in a line, to come when they were called, and to keep a safe distance from bikes and scooters and other things with wheels.

When at last she felt perfectly satisfied with them, she said one morning: "Come along, children. Follow me."
Before you could wink an eyelash Jack, Kack, Lack, Mack, Nack, Ouack, Pack, and Quack fell into line, just as they had been taught. Mrs. Mallard led the way into the water and they swam behind her to the opposite bank.

There they waded ashore and waddled along till they came to the highway.

Mrs. Mallard stepped out to cross the road. "Honk, honk!"
went the horns on the speeding cars. "Qua-a-ack!" went
Mrs. Mallard as she tumbled back again. "Quack! Quack!
Quack! Quack!" went Jack, Kack, Lack, Mack, Nack,

Ouack, Pack, and Quack, just as loud as their little quackers could quack. The cars kept speeding by and honking, and Mrs. Mallard and the ducklings kept right on quack-quack-quacking.

They made such a noise that Michael came running, waving his arms and blowing his whistle.

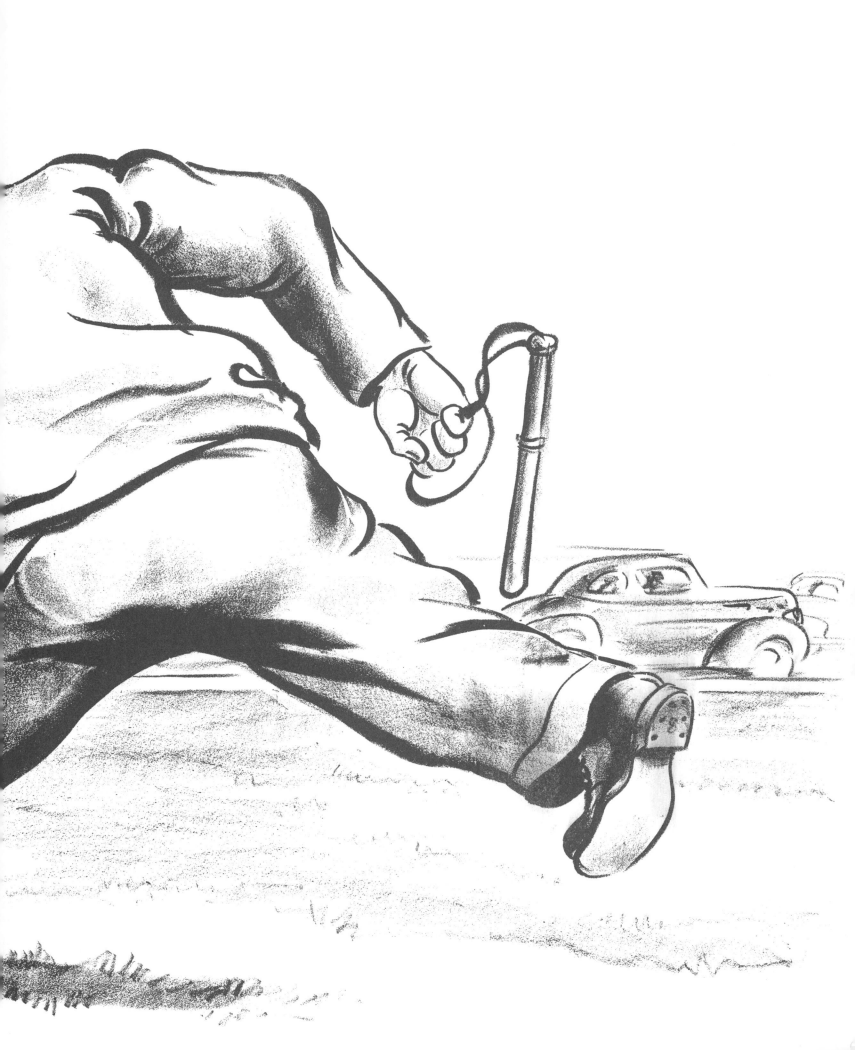

He planted himself in the center of the road, raised one hand to stop the traffic, and then beckoned with the other, the way policemen do, for Mrs. Mallard to cross over.

As soon as Mrs. Mallard and the ducklings were safe on the other side and on their way down Mount Vernon Street, Michael rushed back to his police booth.

He called Clancy at headquarters and said: "There's a family of ducks walkin' down the street!" Clancy said: "Family of *what?*" *"Ducks!"* yelled Michael. "Send a police car, quick!"

Meanwhile Mrs. Mallard had reached the Corner Book Shop and turned into Charles Street, with Jack, Kack, Lack, Mack, Nack, Ouack, Pack, and Quack all marching in line behind her.

Everyone stared. An old lady from Beacon Hill said: "Isn't it amazing!" and the man who swept the streets said: "Well, now, ain't that nice!" and when Mrs. Mallard heard them she was so proud she tipped her nose in the air and walked along with an extra swing in her waddle.

When they came to the corner of Beacon Street there was the police car with four policemen that Clancy had sent from headquarters. The policemen held back the traffic so Mrs. Mallard and the ducklings could march across the street,

right on into the Public Garden.

Inside the gate they all turned round to say thank you to the policemen. The policemen smiled and waved good-by.

When they reached the pond and swam across to the
little island, there was Mr. Mallard waiting for them,
just as he had promised.

The ducklings liked the new island so much that they decided to live there. All day long they follow the swan boats and eat peanuts.

And when night falls they swim to their little island
and go to sleep.